Colly's Barn

For Catherine, Simon, Jonathan,
Susannah, and James
M.M.

To the memory of
Phil O'Connor
I.A.

Chapter One

SOMEONE HAD TO clean out the old barn.
Grandpa had a bad knee and her mother and
father were busy, so Annie had to do it all by
herself. But she wasn't alone. You were never
quite alone in the old barn.

Screecher, the barn owl, looked down at her
from his perch on the beam above her. She
knew that the swallows would be watching her
from their nests high on the roof beams. But
the owls and the swallows were as much a part
of the barn as the walls and the roof and she
paid no attention to them.

It was hot work and smelly too, but Annie
was used to that. After all she had grown up
on a farm, and on a farm there were always
smells of one kind or another. This was no
worse than most.

"Be nice if the cows would learn to clean up
after themselves," said Grandpa from the door

of the barn. "I thought maybe you could do with some water." They sat down side by side on a hay bale. Annie drank until the bottle was empty. Grandpa was looking around him. "This barn, your father wants to knock it down you know," he said.

"What for?" said Annie.

"Old fashioned, he says, and maybe he's right." Grandpa poked the wall with his stick. "Cob, that's just some mud, a few stones, and straw; and it's lasted all this time. Course there's a few cracks in it here and there, but I told your father, it's good for a few years yet."

On the beam above them, Screecher stretched his legs and flexed his talons. Grandpa looked up. "And Screecher, he's been here since the place was built, or his family has. They always nest in the same place. Same as those swallows, they've been coming here ever since I can remember." Grandpa stood up and leaned on his stick. "Makes you think," he said, "thousands of miles they come every year, across the continent from South Africa and straight back to this barn. There's one now." As he spoke, Colly flew in over his head and up to the nest above, fluttered there for a moment and then swooped down again and out the door.

"Look," said Annie, "there's a baby in the nest, you can see its head."

"So you can," said Grandpa. "You can hear it too. I wonder what it's saying."

Annie laughed. "Birds don't talk," she said.

"Not like you maybe," Grandpa said, "and not like me, but they talk all right. We just don't understand what they're saying, that's all. I wonder if they understand us?"

"Course not," said Annie, but it gave her a lot to think about while she mucked out the barn and when you've got something to think

11

about time passes quickly. She never even noticed the evening coming on and she never once looked up at the swallows' nest again. If she had, she would have seen the fledgling swallow perched precariously on the edge of its nest trying out its wings.

Screecher saw the baby bird but did not say anything. Colly was a good mother. She did not need any advice from him as to how to bring

up her family. She
was his friend too,
his oldest friend.
They'd been living in
the barn longer than
any of the other
birds. All winter,
every winter,
Screecher would
look forward to the
day when Colly would

come flying back into the
barn, bringing the spring with her. When Colly
arrived she never rested, not for a moment. She
would build her nest, working every hour of
the daylight. Colly would hatch her eggs and
then fly in and out, in and out, keeping her
family fed, and this year she had to feed them
all on her own. No one really knew
what had happened to her mate. He
just went off hunting one morning
and never came back. It could have
been a car; it could have been a cat.

13

Screecher was just thinking about the cat when he heard her, and then he saw her creeping in through the door. Everyone warned everyone else. "Look out! Look out!" they cried as the cat stalked stiffly past the hay bale and sat down under Colly's nest, her tail whisking back and forth, her eyes fixed on the nest above her.

Screecher knew what would happen, he had seen it all too often before.

Suddenly terrified, Colly's youngest fledgling beat his wings frantically. Then he lost his balance and fell. The cat watched as the baby bird fluttered helplessly down towards the floor of the barn. She knew she just had to wait. There was no hurry, no hurry at all. She wasn't even hungry, she'd already had a nest of mice that day. This bird was for playing with.

Then, Colly came gliding in with a mayfly in her beak. She dove at once, screaming at the cat, banked steeply and came in again. The cat ducked as Colly swooshed by and she swiped the air with a claw as Colly passed overhead. The fledgling was flapping his way to the corner of the barn. The cat crawled after the young bird, slinking along the ground, ignoring Colly's desperate attempts to drive her away.

There was only one thing Colly

could do now. She landed between the cat and her stranded fledgling, and hopped away on a leg and a wing pretending to be wounded. "I've broken it." she cried. "I've broken my wing."

The cat stopped, turned and followed her. A big bird was always more fun to hunt than a small bird.

Screecher sprang off his perch and floated down on silent wings. The cat heard the whisper of wind through Screecher's feathers and looked up. She saw the wide spread of white wings and the talons coming at her, open and deadly. She backed away in surprise. Screecher had never challenged her before.

"Colly," said Screecher, keeping his eyes on the cat as she slunk away. "I'm going to pick him up and put him back in the nest. Tell him to hold still. Tell him not to be frightened."

Screecher's talons curled carefully under and around the fledgling. Then he took off, lifting him higher and higher until at last he was hovering above the nest and could let him go. The fledgling dropped down into the nest and huddled, complaining, in a corner. Colly landed beside him. "I told you you weren't ready to fly yet, didn't I? I told him, Screecher. Wait till your wings are stronger, I said. Wait till tomorrow. But they don't listen."

Screecher shivered. "I think there's a storm coming," he said. "I can feel it in the wind. I better go hunting before the rain comes," and he opened his wings and flew off the beam.

"Screecher," Colly called after him. "Thanks a million. I won't forget it, not ever."

"What are friends for?" said Screecher as he floated out through the barn door and into the dusk.

The road was always the best hunting ground. The shrubs on either side were full of rustling mice and rats. He had a good night of hunting. Five kills he made, but his two scrawny owlets just kept eating and wanted more. The rumble of thunder was coming dangerously close now. He'd been caught out in a storm once before. Once was enough. "I'm telling you, you can't go hunting with wet feathers," he told them, but that didn't stop them from grumbling about how hungry they were.

Chapter Two

ALL NIGHT, AS the storm raged outside, the birds in the barn huddled together in their nests, burying their heads in each other to block out the sound of the thunder. The wind whined and whistled through the eaves, the walls shuddered and the beams creaked and groaned. But Screecher and Colly were not worried. They had been through storms like this before and the old barn had held together.

Screecher thought the worst of it was over. He was peering through a crack in the wall, looking for the first light of dawn on the distant hills, when the lightning struck. In one blinding flash night was turned into day. A deafening clap of thunder shook the barn and a fireball, glowing orange and blue, rolled around the barn and disappeared through the door.

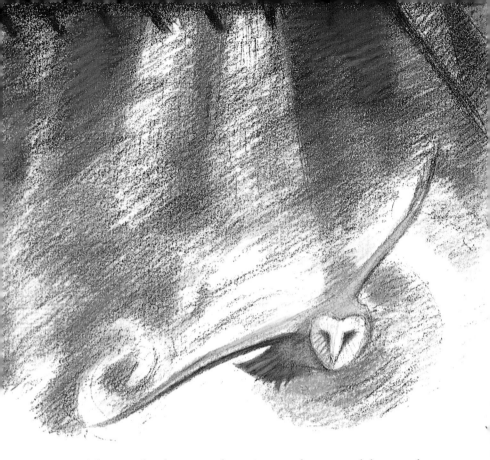

Through the smoke, Screecher could see that the crack in the wall was suddenly a gaping hole and above him the roof was open to the rain.

Grandpa's bad knee kept him in bed the next morning and Annie was at school when her father and mother discovered the hole in the barn wall.

"Lucky it didn't catch fire," said Annie's mother.

"Might have been better if it had," said her father. "One way or another that barn's got to come down now. I've been saying it for years."

"You could patch it up," Annie's mother replied.

Her father shook his head. "Waste of time and money. New modern shed, that's what we need. I'll get a bulldozer in, and we'll soon have it down."

"Grandpa won't like it," she said. "You know how much he likes old buildings. I don't want you upsetting him again."

"It's just a ramshackle old barn," he said. "Anyway, Grandpa won't know until it's all over. He won't be out of bed for a couple of days, not with his knee like it is. Now not a word to Annie, she tells him everything. Thick as thieves, those two."

High above them in the old barn, Screecher and Colly were perched side by side listening to every word. "What'll we do?" said Screecher. "There's nowhere else to nest for miles around; and even if there was, my two fledglings won't be ready to fly for another month or more. I can't move them and I won't leave them. I just won't."

Colly said nothing. She flew off to join the swallows and swifts as they skimmed low over the high grass in the meadow. The message that Screecher and his family were in trouble soon got around. At first some of them refused to help. There was a rumor that Screecher had killed a robin not so long ago. The sparrows and the crows, and there were a lot of them, said Screecher's problems had nothing to do with them, and that everyone had to look after themselves. But all the birds that lived in the barn, the doves, the swallows, the swifts, and the little wren, needed no persuading. After all they had seen Screecher, only the day before, diving down to rescue Colly's fledgling from the cat.

"I've got babies in my nest just like Screecher," said the wren. "If they knock down the barn where are we going to nest next year and the year after that?"

All day long the birds argued, and it was almost dark before they all agreed at last. "Then we'll start work at first light tomorrow," said Colly. "Let's all get some sleep now."

Chapter Three

THE NEXT MORNING Grandpa looked out from his bedroom window at the crowd of birds swirling around the barn. "They must be after the flies," he said to Annie's mother when she brought him his early morning coffee.

"Who knows," she said. "You just stay in bed and rest that knee of yours."

Annie sat down to breakfast in the kitchen. "There's swarms of birds out there," she said. "Just like bees. What are they doing?"

"Who knows," said her father. "Eat up, you'll be late for school."

As she got off the school bus that afternoon
Annie could see the birds still soaring and
swooping around the barn. She ran up the
driveway to get a closer look. Grandpa was
there in his bathrobe. "I wouldn't have thought
it possible," he said. "You see that hole in
the wall? Must have happened in the
storm. They're fixing it, that's what
they're doing."

As Annie watched she saw the wrens, the
swallows, and the finches come flying in with
mud in their beaks. They fluttered briefly at the

wall and flew away again. The crows and
hawks hovered over the roof before landing
with their twigs and straw, and the wren
darted to and fro, her beak full of moss and
lichen. "Your father's not going to believe this,"
said Grandad.

He was right. He didn't believe it. Nor did her
mother. They wouldn't even come out to look.

"You'll get sick, Grandpa," Annie's mother
said. "Go back to bed now."

Annie tried to tell them but they wouldn't
listen to her either. They didn't want to hear
another word about the barn or the birds, not
one word.

"You'll tire yourself out, Colly," said Screecher that night.

"Don't you worry," Colly said. "These wings have taken me south and back five times now. They'll carry me a lot further yet. A few more days and the barn will be as good as new again and then they won't need to knock it down, will they?"

"We need more help with the roof," said Screecher. "I'll fly down to the river tomorrow and ask the herons. They're the experts."

But Colly didn't even hear him, she was fast asleep.

Chapter Four

ANNIE WANTED TO be sure Grandpa was right, so all weekend she stayed and she watched the birds flying back and forth. Even Screecher was out flying by day and she had never seen that before. He was fetching and carrying just like all the others. Of all of them though, it was the swallows, and one of them in particular, that worked hardest, swooping down to the muddy puddles and up to the barn wall without a rest. Annie knew now for certain that Grandpa had not been imagining things.

"It's true," Annie said. "What Grandpa says, it's all true." But they still wouldn't believe her. When Annie shouted at them she was sent to bed early. Grandpa came to comfort her.

"There's none so blind as them that won't see," he said. Annie wasn't sure what he meant by that.

Grandpa told her one of his ghost stories, but she could think only of Screecher and the birds in the barn.

She wasn't at all surprised then to see Screecher fly into her dream. He flew in through the window and perched on the end of her bed. There was something in his beak. He let it fall

on her blanket. She sat up to get a closer look.
It was a dead swallow.

"He's going to knock down the barn,"
said Screecher.

"Who is?" said Annie.

"Your father. We heard him, Colly and me."

"Colly?"

"That's Colly lying on your bed," Screecher
said. "I tried to tell her, I told her she'd kill
herself if she worked so hard. She never stopped
– all day and every day. We've got to finish it,
she said, and then they won't have to knock
down our home."

"Home?" said Annie.

"That barn is our home. We've got nowhere else to live. You've got to stop him. You've got to tell your father or else he'll bring in the bulldozer."

"But he won't believe me," said Annie. "He doesn't believe anything I say. You tell him. He'll believe you, he'll listen to you." And Screecher was suddenly gone.

It's a funny thing about dreams, they always seem to finish just as you wake up. There was

a rumbling outside Annie's window, and voices. She sat up and looked out. Her father was standing by a great yellow bulldozer that belched black smoke and he was pointing up at the barn. Annie looked down and saw the swallow lying on her bed. She picked it up. Colly was limp in her hand, her beak half open. Annie never bothered with slippers or her bathrobe. She ran crying out of the house. Grandpa heard her and her mother heard her. Her father heard nothing until the driver of the bulldozer turned off his engine and pointed at Annie as she came running up the path. Her father looked at the swallow in her hand.

"That's Colly isn't it?" he said.

Annie looked at him amazed. "You know?" she said.

"I had a visitor last night," he said. "He told me everything, Annie. He brought me out here to show me the hole they fixed. When I woke up this morning I thought I had been sleepwalking, so I came and had another look. I wasn't dreaming, Annie."

"Neither was I," said Annie.

Grandpa came puffing up the path, with
Mother behind him. "What's going on?" said
Grandpa. "What's that bulldozer for?"

"Oh, nothing," said Annie's father. "Just took
a wrong turn somewhere, that's all. Lost his
way. We all do that from time to time, don't
we Grandpa?"

They buried Colly that morning in the
corner of the meadow under the great ash tree.
If Annie had looked up she would have seen
Screecher perched high above her, half hidden
by the leaves, Colly's fledgling beside him.
They weren't alone. Every branch, every
twig of the tree was lined with
silent birds.

YELLOW BANANAS

Don't forget there's a whole bunch of Yellow Bananas to choose from: